For the
ROCK STAR
in all of us.

by Amie Simmons
Copyright © 2015 by Amie Simmons

MW00954302

Wednesday is my favorite day of the week.

It is the day my Mom and I go to garage sales.

We wake up early with the sun.

Today we went to Mr. Stringer's garage sale.

He lives on TOp of the hill.

I sure hope he has toys and treasures!

I was l**oo**king and l**oo**king for toys
but I did not see any.
And then a **REAL** treasure caught my eye.
Mr. Stringer was STRUMMING a small guitar.
It was **JUST** my size.

I asked him if it was for sale.

He said it was.

I ran to my mom, **BEGGING** and **PLEADING**.

"Mom, I have always wanted a guitar!

I promise I will write songs

for you and for Dad.

I will practice all of the time."

She smiled and said, "Okay."

I walked home so **PROUDLY** with my guitar.

I sang and played as *LOUDLY* as I could

so that Mr. Stringer could hear.

THIS is what I **SANG:**

"Today I found a guitar
I didn't have to go very far,
Now I'm gonna be a big star
I'm gonna play all the way home
and no matter where I roam
I'm gonna bring my guitar.
I'm gonna bring my guitar."

After we got home, my mom **ASKED** that I put my guitar down and help pack for our camping trip.
I am so excited to play my new guitar around the campfire!
When my dad came home from work, I had **ALREADY** packed and made up a new song for him:

"My Papa's at work

And I packed up all my shirts

He's a coming home

And I'm going to sing this song.

We're going camping!

We're going camping!

We're going camping!

So I can play my guitar around the fire."

TODAY WE LEAVE FOR CAMP WOOBEEGOOBEE!

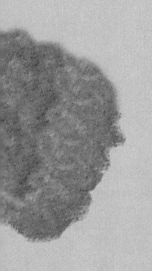

There are all kinds of critters to entertain there. I'm going to have the best audience ever! All of the animals will be talking about me for years to come.

I am going to be **FAMOUS!**

We are going on a canoe ride. I will play for all of the families. I am going to be the most popular boy on the river.

I CANNOT WAIT!

We're here! Papa is building a fire. I unpacked my guitar and I am all ready to roast my s'mores. YUM! Everyone is settling down now and I play another little bed time ditty for the old parents. They really seem to enjoy my music.

"The fire is warm

My belly is full

The fireflies SWARM

And the dream fairies pull

We'll climb in our tents

And zip up the door

To sleep only makes sense

So that tomorrow I can play guitar more."

This morning I played a song for a couple
of friendly critters. They **LOVED** it!

"And the bird goes tweet.
And the bunny goes boing!
The squirrel is silent
Cuz he's chewing on an acorn.
The turtle comes out
And bobs his little head,
My mom calls from the bus
She said put your guitar away
You better listen to what I said."

Put my guitar away? She was
worried that I would lose it on
the river. Luckily, I was able
to convince her otherwise.

When we stopped for lunch I got out of the canoe with my guitar since I said I would never take my hands off of it. I ate lunch and climbed back into the canoe. A couple of people floated by and requested a song. Boy it gets sort of tiring being famous. Still, I went to grab my guitar, but it was not there. I had left it on the SHORE!

TURN AROUND!
EVERYONE!
TURN THE CANOE
AROUND!

He sat me down and said,
"Alright my little rock ★
I started playing the guitar
back when I was your age.
To see people light up when
I would strum on that old thing,
the JOY it brought to their faces. That
is what it was all about for me.
It didn't matter so long as the
music I made helped make at
least one person's day."

I remembered how HAPPY Pa looked when he came home from work. I remembered the animals in the forest and the looks on their faces that I took the time to play for them.

And how could I forget about how happy everyone was on the river singing along and having a jolly old time.

I said, "Mr. Stringer, you're right, I just want to play guitar for my own joy and to share with others. I don't need to be famous."

Upon saying that, Old Mr. Stringer pulled my guitar from his closet!

MUSIC

He returned my guitar! The canoe people sent it to him. My parents asked him to talk to me.

I thanked Mr. Stringer for showing me what music is **TRULY** for. I promised to put a **SMILE** on at least one person's face a day.

And then I sang this song:

"There's nothing better in the world
Than making people smile with music
I said there's nothing better in the world
Than making people smile
When you hear the sound
You'll smile and think
It's what makes the world go 'round."

Made in the USA
Las Vegas, NV
06 January 2022